Eliza Crisp

and the

SNOW | NO SNOW

ABOMINABLE SNOW COMPANY

Published by Clink Street Publishing 2015

Copyright © 2015
First edition.

ISBN: 978-1-910782-79-8
E-Book: 978-1-910782-80-4

For mum

In the middle of an ordinary town,
was an ordinary street.
And in the middle of this street,
was an EXTRAORDINARY house.
This house was
extraordinary,
because it belonged
to Eliza Crisp.
And she was certainly
NOT
ordinary...

Eliza Crisp was the local weather forecaster, and in her garden were hundreds of weather machines, which **hummed and clanked** their weather predictions, day in, day out.

All year long!

There was a machine predicting the wind...

A machine predicting the rain...

But Eliza's favourite machine was the *Snow Globe*, which was special because it made one snow prediction a year. On CHRISTMAS EVE. And this year the Globe was predicting snow.

But there was no snow to be seen!

And even a machine predicting the heat of the Sahara ...

However, our story does not begin in Eliza Crisp's back garden, or with the *Snow Globe*, because at this very moment she was not at home. She was in fact making her way to the local radio station to make her weekly weather predictions. And today was special, as it was Christmas Eve.

And she was very, very, **VERY** late...

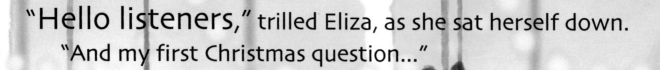

"Hello listeners," trilled Eliza, as she sat herself down.
"And my first Christmas question..."

"Should I plant my onions today?" asked the caller.
"Wait till Tuesday when it will be warmer," replied Eliza.
"Why?" asked the caller.
"Because you won't be able to get the fork into the ground."

"Will it rain on Friday?" asked another caller.
"If the hedgehogs are walking in a zig-zag, then it will be wet," replied Eliza.

"Is it going to be cold in 3 days time?" asked the next caller.
"Do you own a cat?" asked Eliza.
"Yes," replied the caller.
"If your cat sits on the fridge, then it will be VERY cold."

ON AIR

"IS IT GOING TO SNOW ON CHRISTMAS DAY?" asked the final caller.
"That's a very good question," said Eliza, who knew it should be snowing by now.

"Why do they walk in a zig-zag?" asked the caller.
"Because they hate puddles and have to walk around them."

Before Eliza could answer, her show ran out of time "Must go," said Eliza, and she ran out of the studio.

Later, back home, Eliza was inspecting the Snow Globe when Frazzle began to bark. "Our guest has arrived," said Eliza. "Off you go."

Frazzle ran towards the garden gate and jumped through the specially made dog-flap.

As he ran towards her, there was a loud e x p l o s i o n in the back garden.

"Oh no! Not again!" sighed Amy.

On the other side, Eliza's niece, Amy, was walking towards the house. "FRAZZLE," she yelled.

In the back garden, Amy found her Aunt covered in sand.
"Are you alright, Aunty?" asked Amy.
"Perfectly fine," replied Eliza, "But I'm afraid
we have a bigger problem to worry about."
Eliza looked up into the clear blue sky which should
have been full of snow clouds.
"All the signs say it should be snowing."

"Look! The robins are facing south, which means snow has arrived."

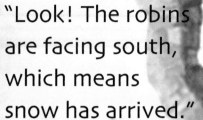

"And the snow weed has a layer of snow on it, a definite sign that there should be snow."

"And I've checked the Snow Globe, which is never wrong. There must be a problem with the snow. Come along, Amy."

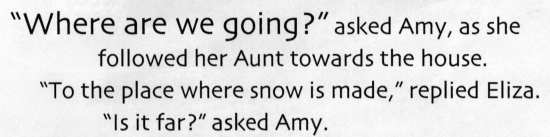

"Where are we going?" asked Amy, as she
followed her Aunt towards the house.
"To the place where snow is made," replied Eliza.
"Is it far?" asked Amy.
"Just the South Pole," said Eliza.
"But that's MILES away," said Amy.
"We'll never get back in time for Christmas."

"Then we'd better get a move on,"
replied Eliza.

With Amy's help, Eliza began to pack for the journey.
"Aunty, how are we going to get there?" asked Amy.
"Oh! I'd forgotten about that," replied Eliza.
She picked up an old catalogue and turned
to the adventure department.

"Ah! This will do."

Eliza picked up the telephone and dialled the number on the front of the catalogue. "I would like to order the Christmas special."

"Delivery now, if you please."

Within a few seconds, there was a loud **screech** followed by a soft **thud!**
"Our transport has arrived," said Eliza.

Amy ran to the window and looked outside. There, tied to the gate, was a huge red balloon.

"It's a big balloon, It's a big balloon!"

screamed Amy. "Perfect," said Eliza. "Time to get the basket outside."

It wasn't long before they were ready for take-off.
"All set, my little adventurer?" asked Eliza.
"All set," replied Amy, importantly.
Eliza untied the rope and the balloon
began to climb up into the air.

"The South Pole, here we come."

As they headed south, they watched dolphins swimming in the blue sea...

And followed birds flying to warmer climates...

They floated down a great golden river...

And witnessed the eerie **Southern Lights**

The next morning, Amy noticed something was different. The landscape had turned white.

"SNOW"

yelled Amy excitedly.

But Frazzle wasn't looking
at the snow and began to bark.
Eliza peered through the telescope.
"I know what you can see."

"Time to land."

As soon as the balloon landed,
Frazzle leapt out of the basket
and ran towards the furry creature.
"COME BACK!" yelled Amy.
"Don't worry," said Eliza, "That's Berty.
He owns the Abominable Snow Company."
"That's me," chuckled Berty.
"Your snow problem is
my snow problem."

"And we have a
BIG
snow problem,"
replied Eliza.

"Did I send the wrong snow?" asked Berty.
"You didn't send ANY snow!" replied Amy.
"I didn't?" said Berty. "Oh dear!"
"Can you help us?" asked Eliza.

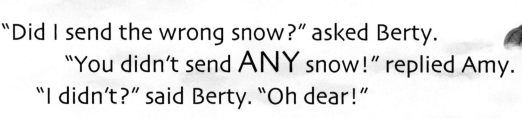

"There's no snow problem that can't be solved," said Berty.
"Everyone, jump into the tractor."

They were soon speeding across the snowy landscape. As they neared a mountain, Berty pressed a big RED button on the dashboard.

"You'll like this bit," said Berty.

Slowly, a door began to open on the side of the mountain.

"Wow! A secret door," said Amy.

"And the next bit is even better," said Berty,
as they disappeared into the mountain.

They were now **_zooming_**
through a long icy tunnel
which descended
deeper
and deeper
and deeper
into the mountain.

Suddenly, Berty stopped the tractor.
"We have to walk from here," said Berty.

It wasn't long before the tunnel opened up
into a **HUGE** ice cave.
"Welcome to the Abominable Snow Company," said Berty.
"Every snowflake in the world comes from here."
"It's **amazing!**" said Amy.
"We'll have to hurry if we're going to get
any snow to England," said Eliza.
"Don't worry," said Berty.
"We have plenty of time."

As they walked through the cave, they saw different types of snow in development.

There were
10 sided
snowflakes,
designed to
travel *FASTER*.

And **sticky snow,** designed to help build **bigger** snowmen.

Non-melting snow, designed for **HOT** countries.

When they reached the English Snow Department, Berty began checking his paperwork. "The snow must have gone somewhere," said Berty. "I don't think it went anywhere," said Amy, pointing to a chart. **"Oh no!"** said Berty,

"I used last year's snow-chart!"

"Is it too late to send any snow?" asked Eliza.
"If we use the 10-sided snowflakes, you shall have your snow," said Berty.
"Time to start up the **snow-dial**."

As the cave went into a state of emergency, Amy noticed Frazzle had disappeared!

SNOW CHART
2014
Egypt snow
Canada snow
Mexico snow
UK snow

Whilst trying to find Frazzle,
Amy wandered into a huge ice-dome.
In the centre was a giant snow-dial,
which Frazzle was climbing up!
"FRAZZLE, COME BACK!" yelled Amy.
But Frazzle had other things on his mind.

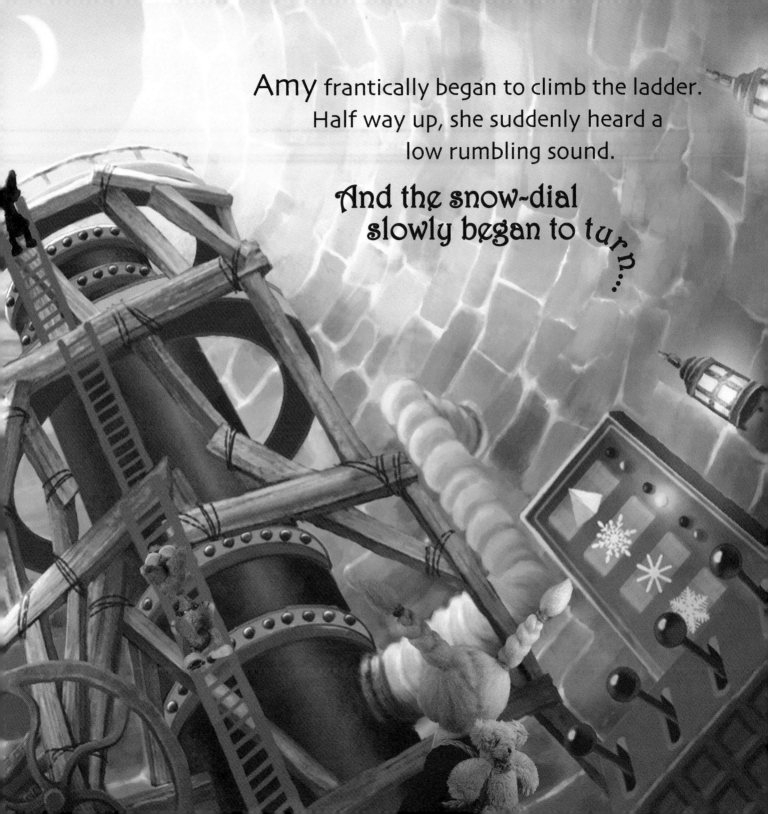

Amy frantically began to climb the ladder.
Half way up, she suddenly heard a
low rumbling sound.

And the snow-dial
slowly began to *turn*...

Just as Amy reached the top
of the ladder, Frazzle jumped
over the Snow-Dial...

As Amy threw Frazzle to safety,
the snow-dial made a loud

ROOOARRRR!

"HEEEEELLLLP!"
screamed Amy, as she was
calapaulted up into the sky
with the snow cloud,
heading for England.

Eliza and Berty were celebrating with a cup of ice-tea when Frazzle ran in and began to bark at the screen next to them.
"What is it, Frazzle?" asked Eliza.
She turned to the screen and saw Amy on top of the snow cloud.

And she was starting to SINK!

'We need to get to the balloon right away!" said Eliza.

"There she is," said Eliza. "I can see her feet."

Eliza launched the
balloon up into the sky,
but Amy was sinking rapidly.
For a moment they lost
sight of her.
"Where's Amy?" asked Berty.

Back safely on the ground, Eliza suddenly realised the time.
"Now the snow is on its way, we must return home."
"Do we have to go?" said Amy, sadly.
Eliza looked at her glum face and
suddenly had a wonderful idea.
"Why don't you spend Christmas with us, Berty?"
"You must come, you must come," said Amy.
"I'd love to," replied Berty.

As the balloon silently drifted along,
Berty began to hear a strange chiming
noise beneath the clouds.
"What's that sound?" asked Berty.
"They're church bells," said Eliza.
"We must be nearly home."

Then the clouds began to clear...

"**There's London!**" shouted Amy.
"And it's 𝕊ℕ𝕆𝕎𝕀ℕ𝔾! "
"Thank you for saving Christmas, Berty," said Eliza.
"You're very welcome," said Berty.